DELETE

IGOR'S LAB OF FEAR

BLOOD SHARK

by Michael Dahl illustrated by Igor Šinkovec

STONE ARCH BOOKS
a capstone imprint

FX: 5-17

Igor's Lab of Fear is published by Stone Arch Books
A Capstone Imprint
1710 Roe Crest Drive, North Mankato, Minnesota 56003
www.capstonepub.com

Cataloging-in-Publication Data is available at the Library of Congress
website.
Hardcover ISBN: 978-1-4965-0456-2
Paperback ISBN: 978-1-4965-0460-9
Ebook ISBN: 978-1-4965-2321-1

SUMMARY: A school field trip. A pit filled to the brim with fossils. A
valuable shark tooth over a million years old. And one bad boy who
doesn't know better than to steal from mother nature. Modern-
day sharks only live in the ocean, but Professor Igor proves that
prehistoric shark fossils can be found anywhere. And where there's
shark fossils, razor-sharp teeth aren't far behind . . .

DESIGNER: Kristi Carlson

Printed in China by Nordica
0415/CA21500547
032015   008840NORDF15

TABLE OF CONTENTS

Go away!

There's no one
at home!

Beware of the shark!

What? Oh, it's
only you.

What did I say? Oh, nothing.

You'll have to forgive me. I've been so busy in my lab lately.

I must be a little tired.

That thing on the wall? That's a shark's jaw.

It has more than two thousand **TEETH**.

Where did I get it?

Well, that's an interesting story . . .

CHAPTER ONE
DEEP DOWN

↓ ↓ ↓

A tall, long-haired boy skateboarded down a lonely road.

The road ended at a tall wire fence.

A sign on the fence read:

PRIVATE PROPERTY

KEEP OUT!

The skateboarder, Taylor, smirked.

"Try and stop me," he said.

Taylor glanced around. No one
was looking.

He grabbed his board and tossed it over the fence.

He gripped the stiff wire with both hands.

Quickly, he climbed over.

Taylor left his board by the fence.

He wouldn't be able to ride it
inside. The ground was all rock and
soft clay.

Taylor saw deep **TIRE TRACKS** in the mud.

Taylor also saw a huge, rocky pit.

The bottom of the pit lay hundreds of feet below the wire fence.

The tire tracks led down to the bottom in a wide curve.

So Taylor followed.

CHAPTER TWO
LOST AND FOUND

The tire tracks had been made by school buses the day before.

Taylor had been on one of the buses.

His class had been on a field trip.

Their teacher had wanted them to dig in the exposed rocky cliffs.

The students were supposed to draw pictures of fossils they found.

"You mean like dinosaur BONES?" Taylor asked.

His teacher shook her head. "Like these," she said.

She showed him a picture of a shell with three segments.

"Trilobites," she said.

"They look like lobsters," Taylor said.

"Millions of years ago, this pit was underwater," the teacher said. "It was part of a prehistoric ocean."

"Ocean?" said Taylor. "Then were there sharks here? Like the Megalodon?"

Taylor had
seen those huge
creatures on TV.

"Maybe," the
teacher said.

"Can we dig
for shark fossils?"
Taylor asked.

"No. Just trilobites," said the teacher.

Taylor sighed. *Why bother looking for
lobsters?* he thought.

He wanted to discover something more exciting.

Soon the field trip was over. All the students walked back to the buses.

A redheaded kid stopped. "I lost my wallet!" he said.

Everyone had to walk back down to the pit to search for the wallet.

After ten minutes, Taylor (found) it.

But he didn't tell anyone.

CHAPTER THREE
THE FIN

Taylor saw a rock.

The rock curved like a fin. It was sharp and smooth.

There's my shark fossil! Taylor thought. *A fin!*

He quickly knelt down next to the rock.

No one was looking, so he buried the wallet in the soft clay next to the fin-shaped rock. He'd come back for it later.

It's not really stealing, Taylor thought.

After all, the money wasn't *for him*. It was for *his mom*.

She had lost her job. They were having trouble paying the rent.

It was getting late. The teacher called off the search.

The redheaded kid cried on the ride back to school.

Taylor didn't look at him.

CHAPTER FOUR
UNDER WATER

Now, Taylor stood at the bottom of the pit.

One edge of the pit was shining like gold. The October sun was setting.

Taylor had to hurry.

He looked around for the fin.

Not many rocks look like a shark fin, he thought. *It should be easy to find.*

Taylor looked and looked. But he couldn't find the fin.

Did someone take it? he wondered.

The light was growing dim.

Finally, Taylor found the fin.
He gasped with relief.

He knelt to pick the wallet up.

Then he saw something else.

Another fin-shaped rock lay a few yards away.

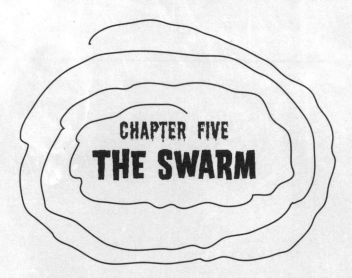

CHAPTER FIVE
THE SWARM

Taylor saw a third fin not far from the first.

Then a fourth. And a fifth.

He stopped to count them all.

There were twelve rocks shaped like fins.

He was sure they hadn't been there before. He would have noticed them.

But where did they come from? he wondered. —Where? —Where? —Where?

CHAPTER SIX
THE SCHOOL

Taylor decided to search near each rock until he found the wallet.

He bent down and touched the first fin.

He pulled back as one of the other fins moved.

The clay beneath his feet began to CHURN and swell.

He felt as if he were riding on his skateboard.

More fins sliced through the clay. They surrounded him. Suddenly, a giant stone shark surfaced.

Mud **DRIPPED** off its smooth body.

It opened its vast mouth.

Taylor saw two thousand teeth and a throat the color of **BLOOD**.

Taylor turned and ran.

He climbed to the top of a rock in the middle of the pit.

A dozen stone fins (circled) around him.

He shouted for help, but his voice sounded strange and distant.

Like if he were deep underwater.

Taylor kept a secret buried . . . and then found an even bigger secret.

Living shark fossils, out for blood.

He barely escaped by the skin of his teeth!

How do I know that?

Well, you see that young man in the back of my lab?

He works here a few nights a week.

Ignore the leash on his foot. I pay him for the work, of course.

After all . . . he owes someone some money. Hee-hee.

PROFESSOR IGOR'S LAB NOTES

Ever heard of the Megalodon? If so, you sure are sharp! But if you haven't, that's okay. The giant shark is a bit long in the tooth — it went exctinct ages ago (probably because it ran out of things to eat, hehe).

These beasts were kind of like the great white shark's bigger, uglier brother. Archaeologists found a fossil of a Megalodon that is 59 feet long! Yikes.

But not all scientists agree on whether or not the megalodon was a separate species. Some think they're just another form of other sharks because they're very similar to the great white shark that still lives today.

Then again, some people think the Megalodon still lives deep within the depths of the ocean, but so far no one has found any convincing evidence. (Probably because they got eaten before they could tell anybody.)

But lots of strange myths have turned out to be real, so who knows!

GLOSSARY

BARELY (BAIR-lee)—almost not possible or almost did not happen

CHURN (CHURN)—move in a circle

EXTINCT (ek-STINGKT)—no longer existing. If a species is extinct, it died out.

FOSSIL (FAHSS-uhl)—something (like a leaf, bone, or footprint) that is from a plant or animal which lived in ancient times that is preserved in rock

MEGALODON (MEG-uh-loh-don)—a huge, ancient shark that is now (probably) extinct

SEGMENT (SEG-ment)—one of the parts into which something can be divided

SURROUNDED (suh-ROWN-did)—enclosed on all sides

SWELLED (SWELLD)—grew larger than normal

TRILOBITE (TRILL-oh-byte)—an extinct, insect-like creature that can commonly be found as fossils

VAST (VASST)—very great in size or amount

DISCUSSION QUESTIONS

1. Do you think Taylor is really working for Igor by choice? Can we trust Professor Igor? Find clues to support your answer.

2. How do you think Taylor went from being surrounded by sharks to Igor's Lab? Can we know for sure?

3. Do you think there is a moral to this story? Why or why not? If so, what is it?

WRITING PROMPTS

1. Do you think Taylor is a bad person or a good person? Do you feel sorry for him at any point in this story? Why?

2. Write a background story for Professor Igor. Who is he? Where did he come from? What does he want? Write about it!

3. What happens next in this story? You decide! Write another chapter to Taylor's tale from Taylor's perspective. Does he escape Igor's lab?

AUTHOR BIOGRAPHY

Michael Dahl, the author of the Library of Doom, Dragonblood, and Troll Hunters series, has a long list of things he's afraid of: dark rooms, small rooms, damp rooms (all of which describe his writing area), storms, rabid squirrels, wet paper, raisins, flying in planes (especially taking off, cruising, and landing), and creepy dolls. He hopes that by writing about fear he will eventually be able to overcome his own. So far it isn't working. But he is afraid to stop, so he continues to write. He lives in a haunted house in Minneapolis, Minnesota.

ILLUSTRATOR BIOGRAPHY

Igor Sinkovec was born in Slovenia in 1978. As a kid he dreamt of becoming a truck driver — or failing that, an astronaut. As it turns out, he got stuck behind a drawing board, so sometimes he draws semi trucks and space shuttles. Igor makes his living as an illustrator. Most of his work involves illustrating books for kids. He lives in Ljubljana, Slovenia.